THE GATHERING

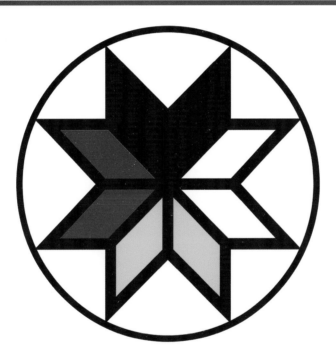

STORY BY **THERESA MEUSE**   ART BY **ART STEVENS**

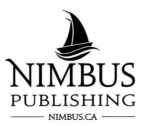

NIMBUS
PUBLISHING
— NIMBUS.CA —

Nimbus Publishing Limited
3660 Strawberry Hill St, Halifax, NS B3K 5A9
(902) 455-4286 nimbus.ca

Printed and bound in Canada
Design: Heather Bryan
NB1058

Library and Archives Canada Cataloguing in Publication

Meuse, Theresa, 1958-, author
The gathering / story by Theresa Meuse ; art by Arthur Stevens.

Issued in print and electronic formats.
ISBN 978-1-77108-466-6 (hardcover).—ISBN 978-1-77108-475-8 (PDF)

I. Stevens, Arthur, 1970-, illustrator II. Title.

PS8576.E887G38 2018   jC813'.6   C2016-908018-8
                                     C2016-908019-6

The eight-point star represents the Mi'kmaw Nation, and the four colours are used by many First Nations peoples in Canada.

Nimbus Publishing acknowledges the financial support for its publishing activities from the Government of Canada, the Canada Council for the Arts, and from the Province of Nova Scotia. We are pleased to work in partnership with the Province of Nova Scotia to develop and promote our creative industries for the benefit of all Nova Scotians.

Alex had never been away from her parents. She loved her cousin Matthew and her aunt and uncle, but was worried about being somewhere new without her mom and dad.

Soon she would be leaving with Matthew and his parents to attend her first spiritual gathering.

In Alex's Mi'kmaw First Nation language, the gathering is called a *mawiomi*, which means "the gathering of people."

It would last four whole days.

After a long drive, Alex, her cousin, aunt, and uncle finally arrived. They parked near the edge of a big field beside the woods. From there, Alex could see a lot of people, cars, and tents. She saw teepees set up in the field and noticed they didn't look like the traditional wigwams she was use to seeing.

She heard drumming and saw smoke off in the distance. She had never seen anything like it before.

Her aunt and uncle began unpacking their camping gear. "Alex," her aunt said when they had finished, "your uncle and I have to help cook the feast today. Matthew will show you around."

Matthew was five years older than Alex and had been to many gatherings.

"You'll be okay, Alex," he said. "You don't have to do anything you don't want to do."

Alex smiled at her cousin and looked toward the sky.

"Where is that smoke coming from, Matthew?" she asked.

"The Sacred Fire," he replied, taking her hand. "Let's go there first."

As they walked, Matthew explained how the Sacred Fire would be lit for all four days of the gathering. A Fire Keeper would be there the whole time to keep it going.

"People go to the Sacred Fire to pray," said Matthew. "We must show respect to the fire and to anyone there."

When Alex and Matthew arrived, the Fire Keeper smiled and welcomed them. He showed them a bowl filled with small pieces of grass and leaves. "These are the sacred medicines," he said. "Placing them in the fire is a way to say thank you to the Creator. The smoke helps carry your prayers."

"I can't do that!" said Alex. "My parents told me to never go near a fire."

"Don't worry," said Matthew. "We won't go so close that you'll get hurt."

Alex wasn't sure, but she reached into the bowl and took some of the sacred medicines. The Elder explained they were sweet grass, sage, cedar, and ceremonial tobacco.

Feeling less afraid, Alex held Matthew's hand and walked with him to the fire. The Elder taught her to hold the medicines in her left hand because it is closest to her heart. As Alex carefully placed her medicines in the fire, it made a crackling sound that made her smile.

The Elder smiled too. Matthew and Alex thanked him for his help. "We'll come back to the Sacred Fire later in the evening," Matthew told Alex.

In the distance, the drumming got louder.

Matthew and Alex began walking toward a drum being played by a group of men.

As they got closer, the drumming got even louder. Alex placed her hands over her ears. Loud sounds always frightened her.

She stayed very close to Matthew as they joined the group of people watching the drummers. Some were dressed in beautiful coloured material decorated with beads and feathers, known as regalia. Others wore plain clothes like she and Matthew. In the crowd, Alex saw other children, and they looked like they were having fun listening. Slowly, she took her hands from her ears.

Matthew saw how brave Alex was being. He told her that drumming was very important to their culture.

"The Elders teach us that the beat of the drum is like the heartbeat of Mother Earth," he said. "When a baby is growing in its mother's belly, hearing her heartbeat makes the baby happy. In the same way, when we hear the drumbeat, it reminds us of the things that make us happy about Mother Earth."

"You mean like seeing and hearing the birds and animals?" asked Alex.

"Yes!" said Matthew. "And seeing the trees in the forest, smelling the pretty flowers, and collecting shells on the beach."

Alex smiled. There were so many things that made her happy about Mother Earth.

The drummers began to sing a song in the Mi'kmaw language. Alex didn't know the meaning of the words, but she still enjoyed hearing the song.

People formed a circle around the drummers and started dancing to the beat.

Matthew asked Alex if she wanted to dance too. Alex was about to say no—but just then, a girl about her age grabbed Alex's hand and started to dance with her. Alex smiled as she felt her feet move to the rhythm of the drum. Soon she and Matthew were having fun dancing.

When the drumming stopped, everyone smiled and some people hugged each other. A lady wearing a beautiful shawl bent over and gave Alex a hug. "You are a good dancer," she said.

Tired from dancing, Matthew and Alex stopped for a snack and a drink and then headed toward a big teepee.

When they entered, an Elder was telling a story. They found a place to sit and listened. The Elder told them about all the things he saw and did during a walk in the forest with his niece. Most of the story was funny and Matthew and Alex laughed a lot.

When the story ended, the Elder said that a Talking Circle would be taking place later in the evening and everyone was welcome to attend.

"What is a Talking Circle, Matthew?" asked Alex as they left the teepee.

"It's a time for people to sit and listen to each other share stories," he said.

Alex was pretty sure she would never be brave enough to join in a Talking Circle.

"There's always an Elder who shows people what to do," said Matthew. "It makes it less scary."

Alex thought about the Sacred Fire, the drumming, and the dancing, and decided that she might be brave enough to go to a Talking Circle—but just to listen. Matthew agreed to take her that night.

Alex and Matthew walked across the field where people were participating in all kinds of traditional activities. They watched Elders preparing a moose hide. They spread a liquid mixture onto the hide and used a scraper to remove all the small pieces stuck to it until it was nice and smooth. The Elders explained this was called tanning. The tanned hide would be used for making the covering of a drum just like the one Alex had seen the men playing.

Close by, some women were decorating moccasins. They taught Alex how to sew the beads, and she sewed a beautiful beaded flower onto some leather. She was even allowed to keep it! She put the flower in her pocket, thanking the women who had helped her.

Next, Matthew and Alex stopped to watch an Elder build a birchbark canoe.

"Long, long ago," said Matthew, "First Nations people could tell each others' canoes by the shape."

"Really?" said Alex. "What was different about a Mi'kmaw canoe?"

"Well," Matthew replied, "Mi'kmaw people had to build canoes sturdy enough to use in the ocean. They rounded

the ends and curved the middle of the canoe, called the gunwale. They used spruce roots found underground to tie it together and used a tree-sap mixture like glue to fill in the holes to keep it from leaking. Together, this helped it stay strong against the ocean waves."

Alex brushed her hand along the side of the canoe. It was surprisingly smooth. She hoped she would get to ride in a birchbark canoe someday—and maybe even paddle one.

Nearby, Alex saw another Elder making something. She noticed Alex watching and spoke to her: "I'm weaving together these wooden strips, called splints, to form a basket," she said.

"What type of wood are you using?" asked Alex.

"In this area, we get the wood from the ash trees," she answered.

Then the Elder let Matthew and Alex weave a splint into the basket. Alex was amazed to find that she could do it.

All of a sudden, delicious smells were in the air. "The feast must be ready," said the Elder.

Matthew and Alex gave their splints back to the Elder, who placed them in a pile. As they all left together for the feast, the Elder smiled and said, "If you come back tomorrow, maybe you can try making a whole basket of your own."

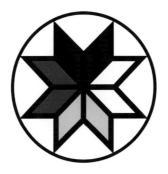

They arrived at the tent set up with lots of tables and chairs. Everyone waited while an Elder said a prayer of thanks to the Creator for the food and thanked everyone who helped prepare the feast. Matthew and Alex smiled, thinking of Matthew's parents. Then the lineup for food started. To show respect to the Elders, everyone allowed them to be served first.

There was plenty of food to eat, like salmon, wild rice, moose meat, and salads. Alex's favourite was a special bread called luski, short for *lu'sknikn* (lou-skin-ee-gan). This was their Mi'kmaw bannock and it tasted so good, she had a two pieces.

With full bellies, Alex and Matthew left the big tent.

"Come on!" said Matthew. "It's time for the Talking Circle!"

Alex watched her cousin run ahead. She began to worry. She had forgotten about the Talking Circle.

Alex caught up with Matthew at the teepee where they had been earlier that day. The same Elder welcomed them to sit in the circle.

Alex recognized the girl she had danced with. She sat down next to her and introduced herself.

"I'm Rachael," the girl replied. Alex smiled and looked at the Elder.

He held a beautiful white eagle feather, and began explaining that it would be passed around the circle, that only the person holding the feather was allowed to speak.

"Everyone else must be respectful and wait their turn to speak," said the Elder. "If someone does not want to speak, they can just pass the feather to person on your left."

Alex was relieved she didn't have to talk.

The Elder told everyone his name, where he lived, and a little bit about his family. When he had finished, he passed the feather to the next person. Alex loved hearing everyone speak, but got nervous as the feather made its way around the circle.

Finally the feather was in Rachael's hand.

"I thought I would be too scared to talk," she said, "and I liked hearing about everyone else." Rachael went on to share about her family, her home, and her cat called Patches.

Alex couldn't believe Rachael had been scared to talk—she was sharing so much!

Finally, Rachael passed the feather to Alex. Alex got ready to pass the feather on to Matthew, but something happened.

Holding the feather made Alex feel brave. She smiled and held it close to her heart.

"My name is Alex," she said, "and I was scared too. I was even afraid of coming to the gathering because I'd never been to one before. But today I learned so many things and here I am talking in the circle. I am so happy I came to the gathering with my cousin Matthew."

Alex passed the feather to Matthew. She'd done it! She'd talked in the Talking Circle. Nobody had laughed or made fun of her.

Alex smiled to herself as she listened to everyone else speak. By the time the Talking Circle was over, it was getting dark.

As they began their walk back to camp, Alex reminded Matthew about going to the Sacred Fire again. Using their flashlights, they found their way across the field.

When they arrived, the same Elder was still the Fire Keeper, and he welcomed them again. This time Alex knew what to do. She and Matthew sprinkled their sacred herbs in the fire. When she heard the crackling sound, Alex thanked the Creator for all the wonderful things she had learned so far at the gathering.

Matthew and Alex wished the Elder good night and headed back to their camp.

Matthew's parents were waiting for them at the tent site.
"Did you have fun today, Alex?" her aunt asked.
Alex told them all about her day. "I gave an offering to the
Sacred Fire, I danced, had luski, sewed beads on leather, saw
leather being tanned, and learned about canoes. I even talked in
the Talking Circle! I'm so happy there are three whole days left.
Tomorrow I get to make a basket for myself!"

Alex's aunt and uncle told her how proud they were of her. They hugged Matthew and thanked him for taking such good care of his cousin. One by one, they entered the tent and crawled into their sleeping bags.

Alex lay in her sleeping bag thinking about her amazing day, and about how glad and brave she was to have come to the gathering with Matthew's family.

She drifted off to sleep with the sound of drums and laughter filling her heart.